hot poems for warm friends

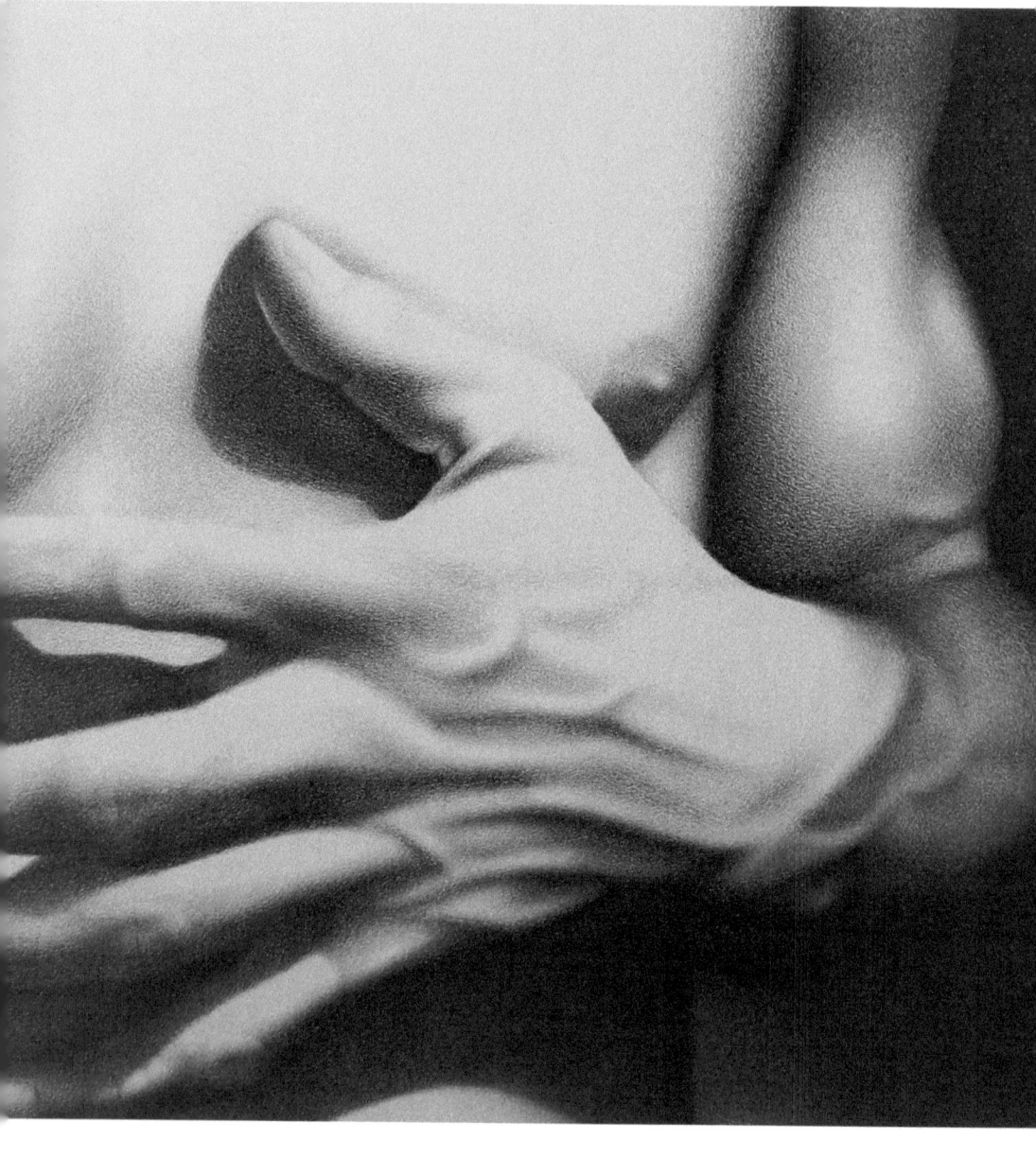

hot poems
for warm friends

George Paris

STARCHAND PRESS
San Francisco

Hot Poems for Warm Friends
© George Paris 2013

Editor and cover design: Charles H. Stinson
Designer: Andrew Ogus
Author photograph © Todd Paris 2008

© Starchand Press 2013
1890 Bryant Street, Suite 300
San Francisco, CA 94110
www.StarchandPress.com.

ISBN 978-0-9858515-0-7

table of contents

editor's note

George Paris came out as a gay man in his 70's. I met
him at a men's retreat at Wildwood in Northern Cali-
fornia, where he recited from memory Howard L.
Chace's "Ladle Rat Rotten Hut" — a hilarious word-
substitution mangling of "Little Red Riding Hood"
(www.justanyone.com/allanguish.html). The audience
howled in laughter, bellies clutched, tears streaming
down faces. I suppose I should mention that he did
this as his alter ego, "Edna May Stumble" and wearing
a red sequined dress, blonde wig, and high heels?

George loves wordplay. He tosses out spoonerisms,
plucks words from conversational streams for amused
examination, and mercilessly drops terrible puns. But
there is far more to him than humor: He is a gentle-
man who plumbs deep topics with open and emotional
honesty.

But poetry is his favored means to examine past and
present. In this short volume of poems he examines
the erotic as something familiar yet new, and illumi-
nates the urges of adolescence with decades of wisdom
and respect.

It has been a great pleasure to work with George, with
book designer and artist Andrew Ogus, and with all
the gifted artists who contributed illustrations for the
poems.

Charles H. Stinson
2012

biographical notes

Born in Lane County, Kansas, George Paris entered school at the start of the Great Depression and the Dust Bowl era. His farmer parents survived for a full decade without income; his younger brother and grandson still farm the same soil.

Mr. Paris received degrees from Southwestern College in Winfield, Kansas, Vanderbilt University in Nashville, Tennessee, and Union Theological Seminary of Columbia University in New York City. He was ordained in the United Methodist Church and served in the ministry until 1970. His late wife, Velma Paris, served as a commissioner of Shawnee County. George and Velma Paris raised five children; the family moved to Topeka, Kansas in 1964.

Mr. Paris has been an artist, an actor, a clergyman, a ceramicist, a teacher, a prize-winning writer of poetry, fiction and non-fiction. He has narrated a CD of stories about growing up in the Dust Bowl years in Kansas, and has written a novel and a play. He served on the staff of the Topeka and Shawnee County Public Library for nearly two decades, and continues to volunteer there. He is a member of the Saturday Night Literary Club and Vice President of the Kansas Authors Club. He is the president of the Saint Andrews Society whose members are mostly of Scottish birth or descent and, of course, wears his kilt to those meetings.

introduction

I began writing seriously after the death of my wife in 1997. Most published poets have gone through one or more university English departments. I was an art major, who got sidetracked into a degree in theology. I do not regret those degrees, for they were the best liberal arts exposure I could have received, but they didn't teach me much about creative writing.

I have learned the art of poetry by writing poems and am still in the process of learning. Writing poems gives the brain a profound workout, and it is a workout I have loved for the past decade.

For this volume I wanted to write poems to share with gay friends. Some I have shared with both straight and gay men and women, but for the most part these are intended for gay eyes. If other eyes fall upon these lines and find them an interesting, entertaining, or perhaps beautiful glimpse, I will feel blessed.

It has been a great pleasure to work with Charles Stinson in the production of this book. I am deeply grateful for his thoughtful comments about my poems and his skills in planning the book and bringing it into reality.

George Paris
September 2011

hot poems for warm friends

the gay poet

I write poems because I'm gay.
Is there a better reason?
Poetry is a crazy word game
if you try to play it straight.
So I write about gay men,
about the sex they enjoy,
the lover they find best.
I know what those men feel
and feel what they know.
I can write that down so tenderly
and they can't tell I'm there at all,
in their pillowed bed,
or on that leather couch.

Oh, I don't interfere with what they do
or how they love — what turns them on.
And they don't know
I'm there to hear their heavy breathing,
their sweet moans and groans.

Yes, I'm a voyeur — you've got that right,
but, in a sense, participant.
And therein lies the poetry —
pure poetry — naked and divine.
Gay lovers, I'm with you!

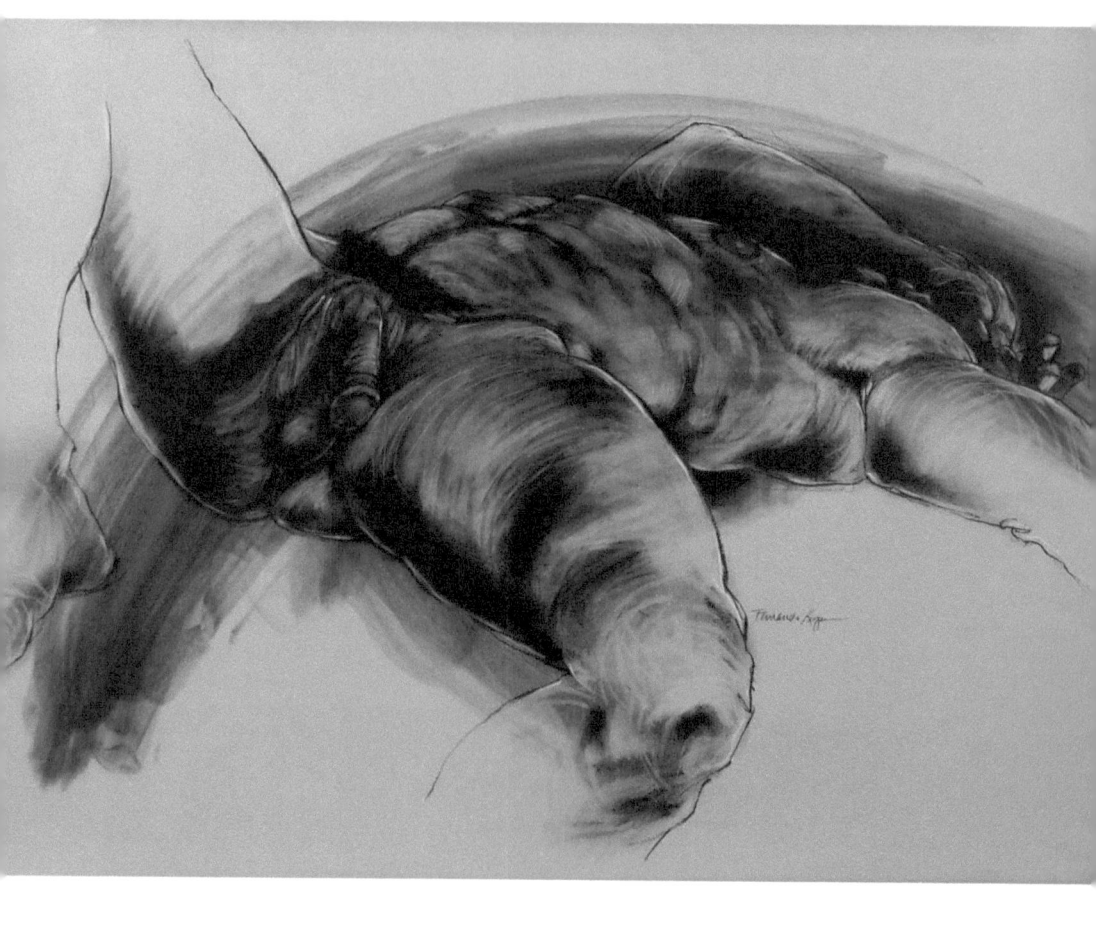

my poems: a reliquary

My poems are an unopened reliquary
containing the clean white bones of my life.
Seemingly sacred, they are simply images,
the only remains of what is the essential me.
Here, the osseous matters lie,
available for anyone
who really wants to look at who I am.

I've often gambled on what I thought
people might understand, appreciate and love.
Misjudgment plagued my lyrical odes.
You will note lines therein revealed
the sin tax owed occasionally,
because of word games played carelessly.
Perhaps I was obfuscating on thin ice.
I dared not *tell* what my brain birthed.
Instead I tried to *show* myself subtly, cleverly,
and ended with far too many adverbs.

But I can't hide in subtle cleverness.
All extra stuff dissolves to show the real me.
Poetry is not an easy ride. It gives the brain
a workout quite profound, peeling off
all fat and flesh around the skeletal frame.
Much of my life now lies inside this box.
But not many people will
stop to open the reliquary,
or examine the bones
because it's labeled "poetry".

trousers

Slacks were all I wanted that fall day.
But he seemed wiser — an adviser.
He, congenial graduate, and I, a freshman.

He was cocksure clothing salesman,
and I, his naïve opportunity.
He used finely honed sales pitch —
and queries about
college dorm life, especially my roommate.

He said nothing alluding to fornication,
but escorted me to a lower level
to try on hottest merchandise,
took my body measurements,
concentrating on the inseam.

He was all help in choosing the proper pair,
but I thought it quite queer when
he followed me into the changing room,
where he changed from salesman into lover.
The man undressed me, commended me for having
an instantaneous, shameful frontal extension!

A marvel at putting me at ease,
he knelt before me, worshipped me,
took my embarrassment in his mouth!
I couldn't believe this adventure —
the most sensational I'd ever known.

Nothing comparable had ever happened
in my bland Christian life. I should
not let him do this sinful thing,
so with my crescendo coming on,
I cancelled intimacy, pushed his head away,
only to mess up his face!

Got him smack dab in the eye,
because why would anyone
want to taste the stuff? Oh yeah!
What I learned in college that year!

dad's opinion

He's a good kid, George is.
He's alright, I guess. Gets good
grades in school, gotta admit that,
but I just don't get him. He's kinda weird.
Gets that from his **Mama**. He wants
to hang around the house all day
like his sisters do. He'd take up sewin'
and crochet and all that stuff if we'd
let him. He don't like to hang around
with me. Don't know why.
I can sure use him helping to repair
the combine, but he's not much use
out here with machinery.
Can't bend balin' wire without breakin' it.
And he don't like to get his hands dirty.
Now when it comes to milkin' cows
he does better than his brother.
He strips them tits plumb dry like they
should be. But he's kind of a sissy boy.
His hands ain't big like they ought to be.
He'd rather wash and dry dishes than
work outdoors. Lately he's takin'
to paintin'. Does a pretty good job
of copyin' those calendar pictures,
but I ain't gonna pay for no art lessons.
No siree! Don't care how good he gets.
It'll never earn him a dime.
Gotta teach him to work. Next year
he'll be big enough to run the tractor.
He'll just have to get over bein' a weaklin'.
He's gotta grow up to be a man,
not one of them queers!

the discovery of nature

Alone on a vast acreage,
a boy drives his father's tractor,
but the world catches his eye
and causes him to wonder.

Why grasshoppers spit tobacco juice
when there's no tobacco within a thousand miles?
Why the meadowlark's song is so brief
one can never catch the tune?
Which is louder — the tractor, or the roar of wind?
Why blossoms of the milkweed must be plowed under?
Why sunflowers turn their faces to the sun?
Why pesky gnats fly only in one's face?
Why is it a sign of rain when flies bite hard?
Why chicken hawks eat bunny rabbits?
Why animals breed in front of us
without getting embarrassed?

There is lots of nothing there
beneath the hot and cloudless sky,
yet the boy sees and wonders.

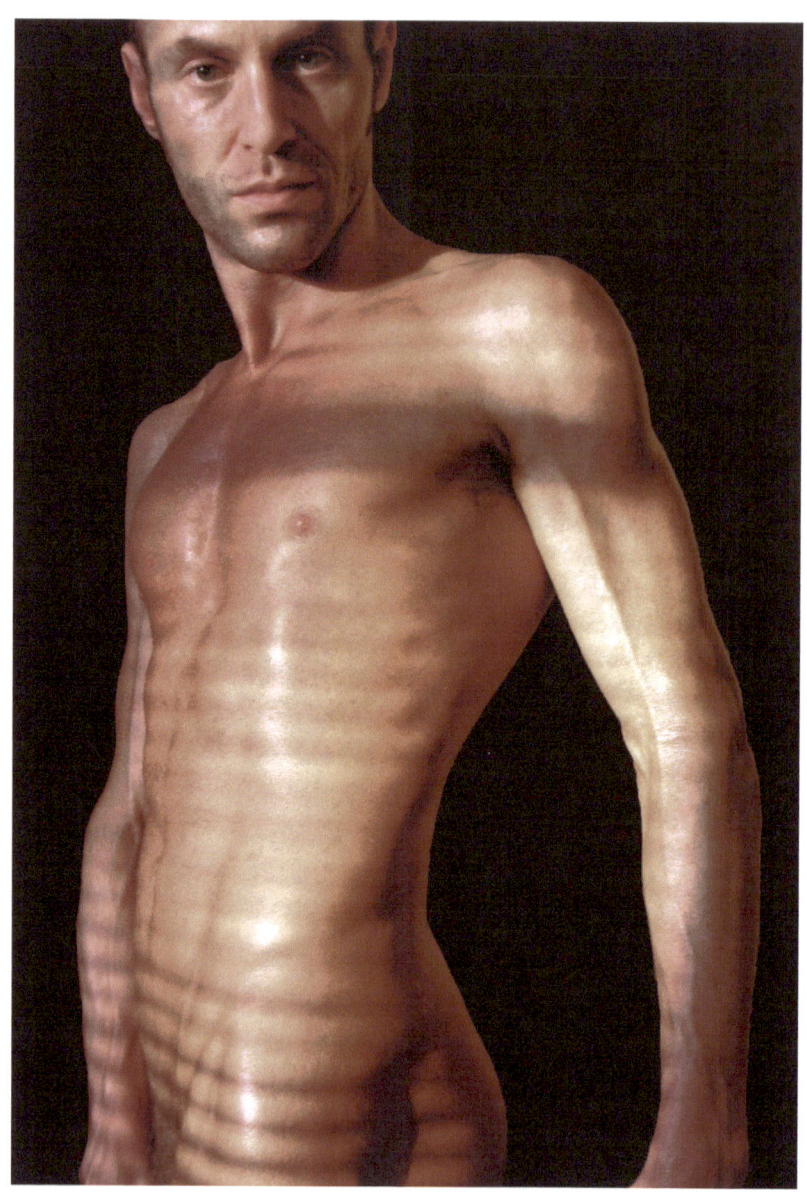

blown out of the water (1948)

There in the old YMCA, he watched me into manhood.
Swimsuits forbidden, did I go there to practice sidestroke?
He stood alone in the shower across the room.
Somewhat older than me, he kept glancing my way,
and finally turned to smile at me and show me his.
I confess to being fascinated as his grew.
Cock-eyed, I hurried past him to the pool, thinking he'd forget.
He followed, for mine had disobeyed, expanding exponentially.
This wasn't standard procedure, was it? Swim it all away!
Purify those thoughts in this holy water for Christian men!
If only I could swim! I didn't know the crawl, but like a dog
I paddled in the shallow end, the safe end — not the end.
Out of breath, I grasped the edge and stood waist deep,
hiding my private life beneath in dark swirls.
Amused, he sized me up across that ocean,
its dancing gay waves laughing at me.
In good farm boy style I returned his grin.
My politeness was my "yes".
How could I have known that my reply meant,
"Come, and have your way with me"?
He dived, swam deep, like sperm whale,
breached in front of me with that lubricating mouth,
then went down to place his smile where I spoke eloquently.
How could I resist? Was I Adam eating that damn apple?
Oh God! He was good to me. How dare this be sin!
I pushed his face away, but not in time.
No longer a boy, I watched the white strings
float away from us.

in heat

Hotter than blue blazes,
no doubt about it!
The temperature climbs
while I search trees
for shades of relief.
Even green is a warm color.
No chance of rain today.
Dog days of August.
Just plain hot. Then

why this furnace of desire?
Fiery memory of your
red-hot kisses still inviting.
Only steamy eye candy
until, naked, you come and
crawl on top of me.
Never mind the sweat.
Bring on your body heat!
I'm cool with that!

the young swimmer

I see him standing there at water's edge,
ready to dive in, yet not quite prepared.
His clothes lie in a pile behind him.
He hesitates as if fearing the water,
but assured that no one is watching.

Lean and thin, his young body
quivers in the afternoon sun
like a newborn colt
having lost sight of his mare.
He cups himself with both hands,
reassurance of his manhood.

What will this baptism mean
if he plunges in over his head?
What direction will he take?
What dangers will he face
in these waters because he's gay?

Having stood there on that spot,
naked and vulnerable, frightened
at the thought of drowning,
why can't we tell him what to do?
Perhaps he knows.

He dives and swims, learning
to survive while swimming.

underwear fantasy

I drool over first one and then the other in the
catalogue. Were it not for the high cost of shipping,
I would gladly undertake all the handling.
I'll order that one. Medium size.

His face, the epitome of male beauty, and those eyes —
soft, brown — twinkle; certain to love me.
He's guaranteed to care about my life — isn't he?
Only twenty dollars in that enhancement bikini!

A perfect body, hairless, no tattoos
or piercings, ready to begin his new life
with me. Oh, gawd yes! I'll take him,
along with what he's wearing, although

I see no need for enhancement.
When he's mine, the wax job
will be history and what he's wearing
will soon be gone.

dancing with the gods

No one has seen God and survived.
Dangerous, they warned,
and it was. Blinded in uncertainty,
I staggered inside my soul,
feeling for a touch of bliss or
conjuring a taste of life eternal.

Breathe, breathe again, he said.
Pant hot. Cry for help.
Listen not to what
my brain would have me know.
Rely on heart's intelligence and enter
now through gates of consciousness.

In full body awareness
divinity took hold.
Through darkness in lightness
I danced in creature wildness
with gods who came
as travel guides to partner me.

Naked, as one we danced,
until I saw through roaring breath,
and knew that touch of golden hands
taking me to the brink
of death so I could live.

a game forfeited

Jeans lowered he stood facing me,
his equipment on inappropriate display
like baseball bat and glove placed
deliberately in my own front hallway.
Here is one poor bastard I don't want
to play catch with. He has already
struck out too many times.
His tattoos are faded like old prayer flags,
skin as wrinkled as crumpled
plastic grocery sacks.

I turn my back on him,
to leave him wanting me, or any man.
I walk away remembering, not him,
but only those games when I was
ignored, rejected, scorned by men
who knew nothing about me, but
saw only a worn-out toy to be pitied
for even wanting to be a teammate.
I wonder: Who, just now, struck out?

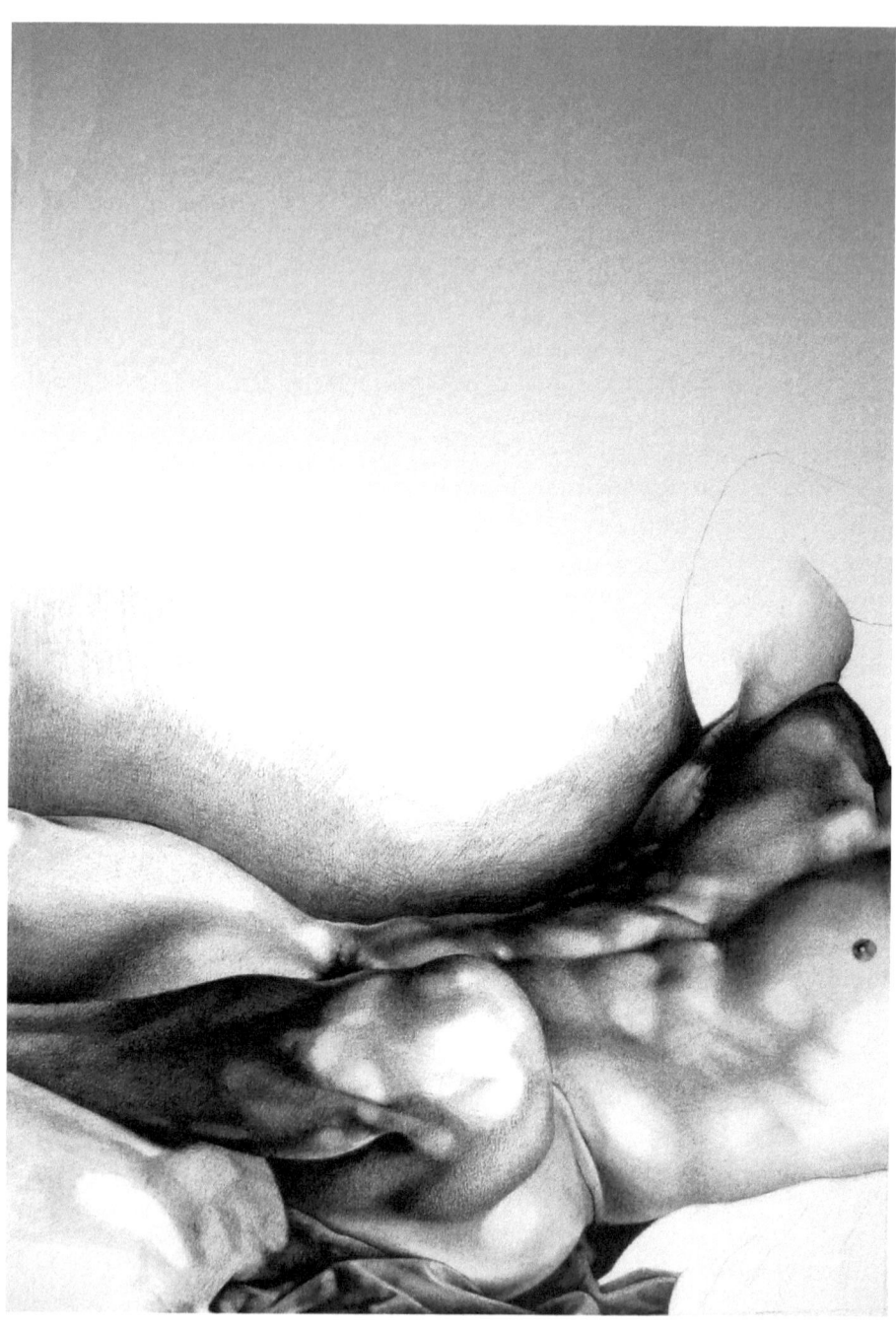

rainstorm

Sky is fucking mother earth tonight.
He lies above her close and heavy.
His balls of cloud hang low,
brushing the valley of her thighs.
His lightning thrusts are answered
by her thunderous moans and shouts.
Passion rules his dark desire,
and she submits to pleasure him.
Their sex continues through the night
with briefest respite here and there.
Ten million wriggling sperm-like drops
seek entrance to some part of earth,
where new life will begin to grow and swell
the belly of her motherhood.
Long and loud their union lasts
until his body moves away,
and leaves our mother bathed in sweat.

She is pregnant with new possibilities.

a balancing act

Now that I'm an octogenarian,
I balance on the equator of my world
that divides young from old, hot from cold.

"It's all a matter of attitude," they say.
"You are as young as you feel."
I have a problem with that platitude.
Some of me feels youthful and some feels ancient.
Too often the venerable, supported by arthritis,
wins the argument and tells my body "ninety-nine,"
although my mind says "twenty-nine!"

I've seen them, shivering in nursing homes,
their eyes empty as the shells
of last year's Easter eggs. They sit alone,
hoping for the visit from the dark prince.
I abhor the look of desperation.
So I seek young men
who enable me to feel unseasoned.
I watch their boundless energies,
the flames in their eyes
like erupting forest fires,
overtaking the continent.
I catch fire with them, love the heat,
living for a while on the hot side of my equator.

the butter knife

Behold the lowly butter knife,
glorious in silver blade and ornate handle,
peerless to observe, but dedicated
to a single, simple purpose: slicing butter.
A distinguished persona in decorous design,
but characteristically, he's rather dull —
a blunt sword useless for any other purpose
(certainly no help in self-defense).
I've seen him dressed in 14-karat handle,
again in mother-of-pearl, or sculpted silver,
handsome and preeminent at
the formal dinner, outshining any other cutter.
Steak knives, on losing their sharp tongue,
cringe in shame when they hear diners say
"These could almost cut soft butter."
They can and will be honed many times.
But the butter knife needs no alteration.
He depends only on that mold of gold
for humble work and peaceful duty.
Those around the table silently admire him
while they take for granted
all other edges. He's, after all,
the best dressed utensil at the table!
The butter knife, though dull of blade,
contains a grace and beauty often needed.
He holds a place of honor in my mind,
as well as *persona grata* at my table.

"Softening"

living after dying

A day will come when my skin will be
too essential to spark wild smell.
My covering is already stretched
too thin to hide purple rivers throbbing.
I will rust like a wasted whisper
when morning is cracked
glass and thin film music.

I will fade like ocean mist and drift
into a home aboriginal
where all things can be
re-learned with happy voices.
Broken crystals will dazzle into
new forms and I'll breathe
those whispers, almost lost,
into carings of vast dimensions.
The rivers will meet to form
a great flow of new mornings
when I embrace infinity.

a love that might have been

You and I could have been
great lovers had we followed
what our hearts told us.
The politics of being gay,
compromise or demise,
was terrifying!

> Would our love have been
> beautiful, or laced with
> agony and scorn?
> Might we have kissed,
> but only in the darkness of
> secret places?
> No wedding bands,
> nor holding hands
> in open airy spaces.
> Forbidden to own a home
> in which our bodies
> could actualize attraction.

We chose to marry,
not each other whom we adored,
but women who befriended us
and bore our children. We did
the safe and honorable thing,
didn't we? With loving faithful
spouses and adorable offspring
we had advantages, didn't we?

But the memory of your long ago
embrace would not erase.

    Death has called our wives and
    we have met to talk of
    what might have been.
    We can no longer be
    the beloved for each other,
    hot and close, legs entwined,
    as if we were twenty-one.
    What or who has changed?

cloud tricks

As if designed by Fragonard,
clouds hang in the sky
all cottony, puffy, pure,
with only a hint of pink.
I watch entranced
while the clouds move
ever so slightly.
On the foggy edge of sleep,
I see a fat little cherub, a putto
Verrocchio himself might have made,
peeks from his soft cover.
He looks directly at me while I stare,
and then, he winks at me!
I swear, he winks and grins!
His Botticelli wings flutter slightly,
then he disappears behind his cloud.

What was that all about?
Nothing but water vapor, I reason,
nothing more solid than air. And yet . . .
I should have winked at him!

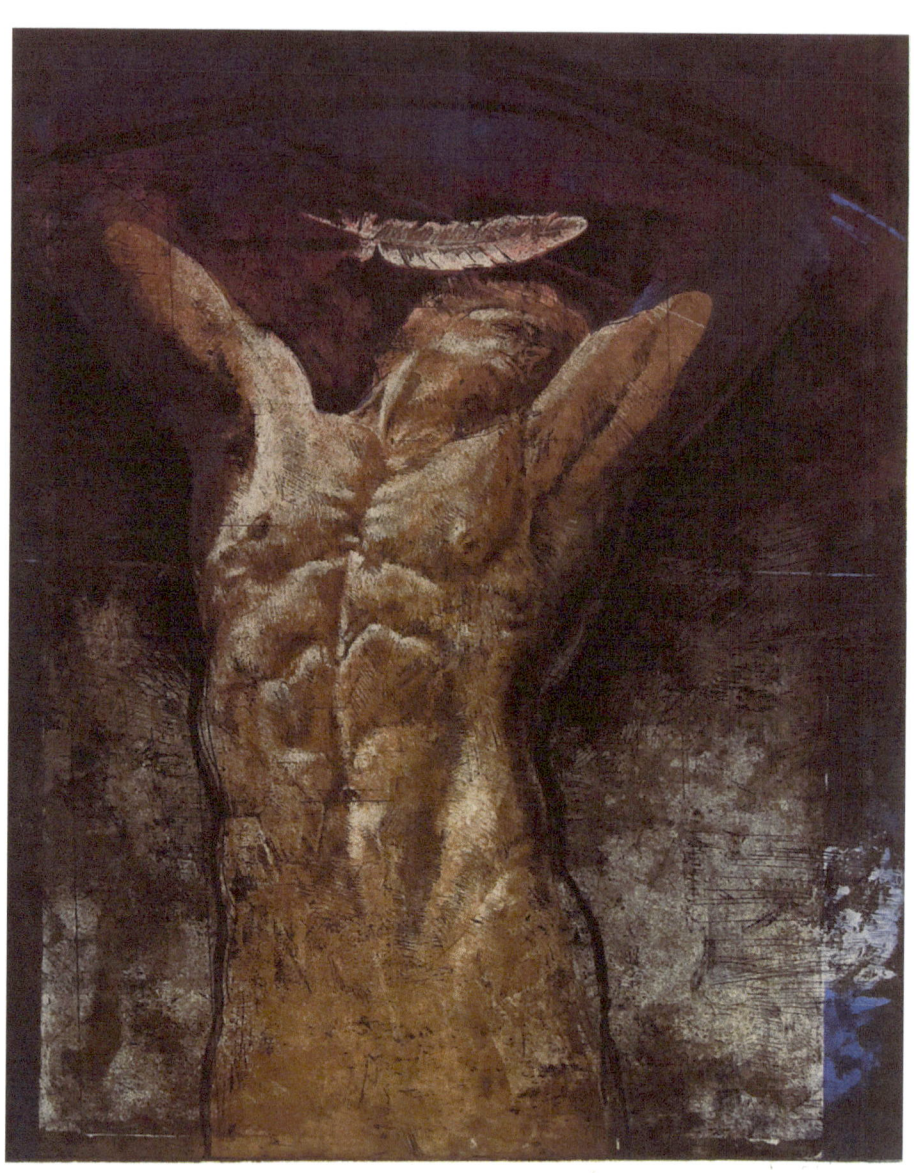

before you touch me

In that between moment
before your hand touches
and the touch itself,
there is much to be discussed.
Yet what is to be said?

As if I knew the difference.

I plot the geometric protocol
of procedural certainty
believing an answer is
somewhere to be discovered.

I'm only plucking goose feathers
from my pillow to get
to the bottom of things.
The touch will happen,
the connection made.

Divine intent would be
no more perfect.
Meaning comes
with your kind hand.
No need to understand.

rain dance

Naked, unashamed,
    they dance for hours.
Never tiring, never resting,
    raindrops cavort
on the dance floor
    surface of the pond.
They unite with
    the welcoming body
beneath them,
    making them whole again,
as once they were
    (*as we were*)
before the metamorphosis
    from ocean into rising cloud.

They fall from heaven,
    blessing the earth
(*as we can*),
    fertile and expectant.
Rain: enchanting,
    sexually explicit,
fluid aspects of Eternity.

in praise of ecstasy

"After the ecstasy, there is always the laundry."
Some guy wrote a whole book on the subject.
He insists I must clean up my act,
though I never considered it dirty.
There's more than washing sheets in being clean.

Yes, I will wash the damn sheets,
I will wipe away those pleasant stains
of lingering sensuous joy
and vacuum my emotions, if need be!

But the ecstasy must last.
After bathing, I will
wallow in that earthy mix of living,
feel soil on my hands,
grime on my jeans, sweat on my brow,
the swirls of passion in my loins
with heart brim-full
of tenderness.

I don't want to do the laundry too soon!

a day in june

It would have been that perfect June day,
but a heavy evening was building
like a fermenting, fiery metaphor.
Tornado weather!
I want you here with me,
to share the storm's violence,
our own electric fire brewing
in bed, beneath wind and rain.

Like a flash of lightning,
the phone rings, scattering the beauty
of my daydream, like leaves
driven before a gale. A woman's voice
speaks: "If the sirens sound, would you
mind if I came down and joined
you in your bathroom?" This woman
who lives upstairs — she
doesn't know I'm gay.

I pause, wondering if I would rush
to the door and greet her in the nude
and show her to my sanctuary.
"Certainly! Come on down," I say,
not certain how I'll open that door.
Will I have time to don clothes? I doubt
if my tub can hold two bodies side by side.
Will she be on top? Or will I?

In deciding these matters
we could both be blown away
and nothing would matter,
metaphorically.

a lonely man

In the coffee house, he sits alone,
outfitted as disreputably as possible.
Last shaved, three weeks ago,
long hair uncombed,
piercings he could ill afford.
Hunched over his coffee as if
it were to escape his grip.

Does he know he appears
ready to commit suicide,
or worse, mass murder?

Horrified, I try to look away from
the dark brilliance of his depression,
but his locked expression spreads to me.

I ponder his probable problems:
homeless starving artist — persecuted
gay activist, failing student —
What would he look like,
cleaned and groomed?
Does anyone love him?
When was the last time
he lay in bed beside a lover?
Perhaps I jump to conclusions.
Surely, he has friends.

Were I a psychiatrist, I would
offer my services free, on the spot.
But I am not.
I place my cup on the table
across from him, sit down
and introduce myself.

to allen

I see you lying on that leather couch.
Your jeans pulled down around your thighs —
no underwear in sight. All right!
Your eyes are closed, but you are not asleep;
you're lost in some erotic fantasy.
Your cock is full and hard, as if prepared
for winning the category "Best of Show".
I long to touch your body — run my fingers
through the hair on belly, ribs and chest
and kiss and lick each nipple 'til you shake.
I'd kiss those pouting lips that look so ready
and so ripe and love you 'til you need my love
no more. I see you lying there upon the couch,
exposed, vulnerable, and incredibly sweet.
But I can only watch and dream of you.
Although your pose is clearly invitation to a dance,
it is a dance I cannot make with you.
For I am not the lover that you need.
I must be content to watch you
lying on the couch, and simply smile
and love you, as I do,
but from the aching distance
of a thousand crazy miles.

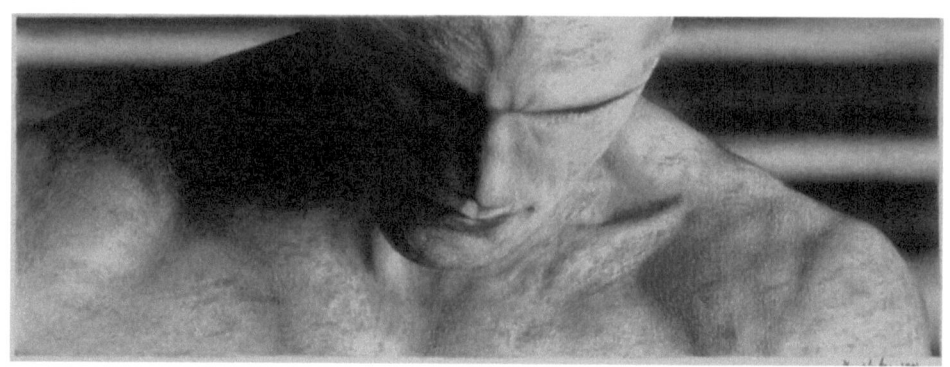

trees like men

The trees this fall are like some
gay men I know. They can't decide
which way or when to turn.
Some stand there half naked,
having dropped their clothes
from off their upper limbs,
their lower parts conspicuously
covered. There are a few completely
nude, buck naked in the open air for all
to behold. Others are flushing red
on one side, green otherwise. Many
trees are yellow, not daring to blush.
I saw two bushes side by side
like ass cheeks freshly spanked
perhaps too much — painfully red!

in praise of nudity

My home is clothing optional,
some of the time — that is, all of the time
when I'm alone, but even when I have guests
of a certain kind. You know, the type
who, like me, just prefer being naked.
Often they're broadening their education,
interested in looking down my torso
to see what my clothes have been hiding.
I just "grin and bare it" as they say.
Well, after all, we were born *au naturel.*
Why not stay that way? Of course, we'd be
arrested if we went about the town disrobed,
and yet I'll no doubt be in one of those
hospital gowns that makes you feel unclad
when I die, so why be a prude about this matter?
I enjoy being nude — nothing half-assed about it.
I eat breakfast, wash the dishes, and actually
shampoo, shave and shower in the buff!
I do house cleaning the same way.
(I confess I wear an apron when frying bacon.)
If we had nothing to hide we'd be less paranoid.
I'm for the unveiled truth, a full disclosure.
Therefore at bedtime after dining out,
I take off all my duds and cuddle up
in bed in my good old birthday suit.
What better way to sleep? Pajamas
would only get tangled up with me.
Three cheers for nudity!
RAW! RAW! RAW!

nocturne

He lies soft,
pillow-borne, naked,
dreaming hard.
Breathing sweetness,
hand nurturing
swelling cock.
Innocence needing
connection.

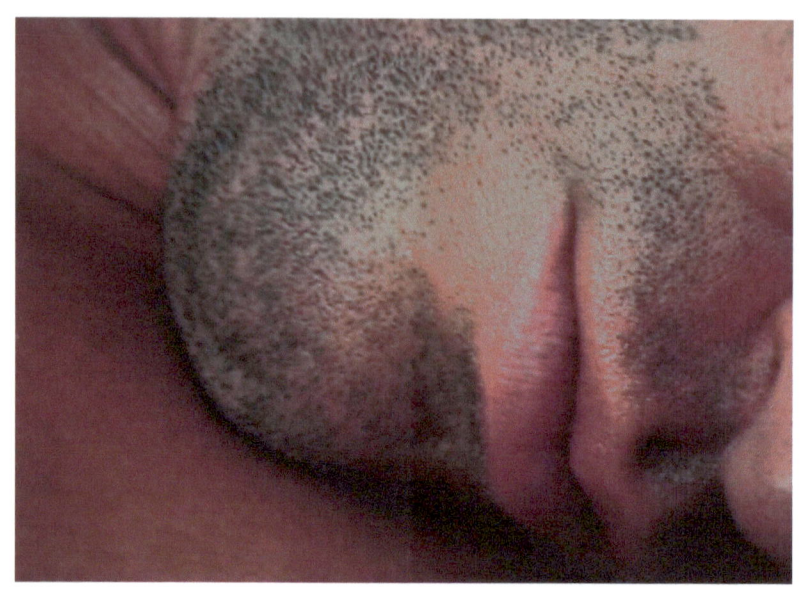

invitation

Your presence is requested.
Distance is not good.
We languish in separation.
Thirsty for kisses,
I hunger for your body,
longing to be one with you,
tasting the honey
of your sweat, the wine
of your kiss. I want you
beside me, beneath me, or
inside me — tonight.
Warm as chocolate,
luscious as ice cream,
hot as prairie fire scorching,
sharp as ice, you move
across my flesh to melt
and trickle down in laughter.
You are all of this and more.
Come, be with me again.
Please accept my invitation,
and allow me to treat you
to a gourmet feast of loving.

cock–a–doodle–do

(any cock'll do)

Hello there, you handsome little dick!
I see you hiding within that crotch.
Come on! Come out to play.
Come alive. I want to see you grow.
You are a noble cock. Come on!
I want to hear you crow.
Become all that you can be.
Live up to your full potential.
Bloom big, strong and full of life.
That's right! Stand tall, erect and firm.
Don't hide your beauty.
Throw back that hood,
allow your head to shine.
Let all of your magnificence emerge.
Produce something of significance.
You were made for love.
Settle for nothing less!

Yeah, you handsome dick,
I love to play with you. When excited
you make me feel so good.
You're at your best,
giving me the utmost pleasure.
As my rod and staff, you comfort me.
I anoint you with oil to honor you
and you respond to gentle touch
as if beside green pastures.

When quiet and subdued,
you grace my body
as its most attractive feature.
You also rise to meet the challenge
of a more rigorous treatment.

I love you, sweet wonderful dick.
I'm so pleased that we have come
to know each other intimately.

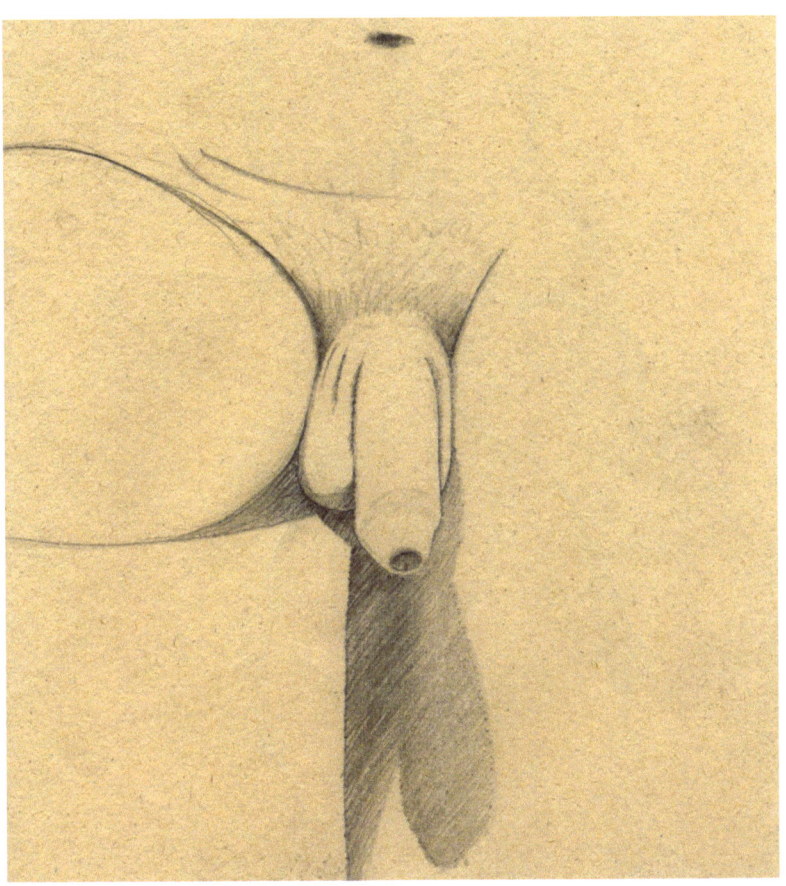

the seducer

His aftershave lotion faded,
but the smile lingered
long enough for intrigue
to settle, sifting down through
synapses of my left brain cortex
until I succumbed to his plan.
A master at cool strategy,
he grinned from within his
leather jacket and kept his eyes
focused on me until
I was without defense, and
yes, so dense, I couldn't see
what was coming.

He wanted me. I wanted him.
But I played hard to get.
He seemed quite fascinating
with that question always on
his face. And he was very cute!
I wondered how he'd kiss.

Oh, what the hell!
Nothing ventured, nothing gained.
I'm easily swayed.
Smiling back at him,
I clinched the deal
as solid as the Kyoto Protocol
without a single signature.

eyes of friendship

Look deep into the candle's flame.
Watch its discomfort as it lurches here and there,
as if it wants to leave in desperation,
but can't escape the wick that gives it life.
It becomes distorted, tentative
with each slight current of air.
Perhaps it fears your steady gaze.

Look deep into my eyes, good friend.
Observe the comfort that's reflected there.
Watch the richness and the love these eyes return.
How steady and unblinking is my gaze.
There is no fear, no need to run,
no desperate wish for someone else.
What lights these eyes is nothing less than you.

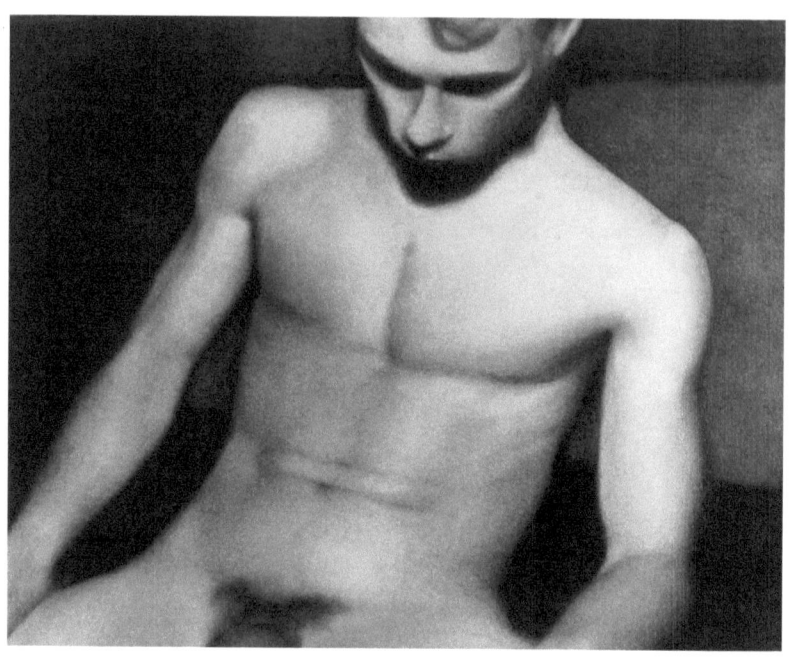

dirt

Between the dirt from whence I came
and the dust I will become,
I will have touched, even swallowed,
great mounds of dirt.
Born on Kansas farm soil
I breathed the dust bowl.

When I became a man,
never certain how or when,
I came to know
the muck of life —
the slime that people throw
at one another.

Such dirt sticks to soul
as well as body, and eats away
at what one hopes to be,
eroding altruism and good deeds,
a filth too nasty
to simply wipe away.

Innocence blessed
the dirt of childhood.
Water washed it off,
but some of the other crud
still clings. Where is the "Mr. Clean"
that prayer was supposed to be?

to joe

I meet you in a place of mystery — the heart.
Coming in from the bedazzled outside,
I do not recognize you at first.
Sometimes difficult to see, inside.
Vigorous walker, this is where you live,
in, and from, the source. Your eyes invite me
to stay. I must accept. Life will be enriched.

We feast on a banquet of delights
in a vast chamber of correlation.
Each course richer, more satisfying
than the previous — savory
between the two of us, not excluding
anyone. Rumi dances in to join us for dessert,
congratulating us on how well we've met.

We join eyes and hands with the poet
to whirl in ecstasy. We are drunk
with the wine of naked sensuality.
Ours is the universe of awareness
of life's playfulness, its tragedy and triumph.
The world is not stage enough.

You move with grace so balanced
as to set Pisa's tower erect. You anoint me
with the tears of your laughter, demanding
that I own my potency. You are unaware
that the feast was of your doing,
yet, because of you, I am at peace.

Buddha joins us, acknowledging in silence
that we have known some part of his vision.
Here, inside the heart, our home, we dance.

limericks

A famous urologist, Phil,
was loathe to prescribe any pill.
Pretending oncologist,
he probed as proctologist,
and gave his male patients a thrill.

———————————

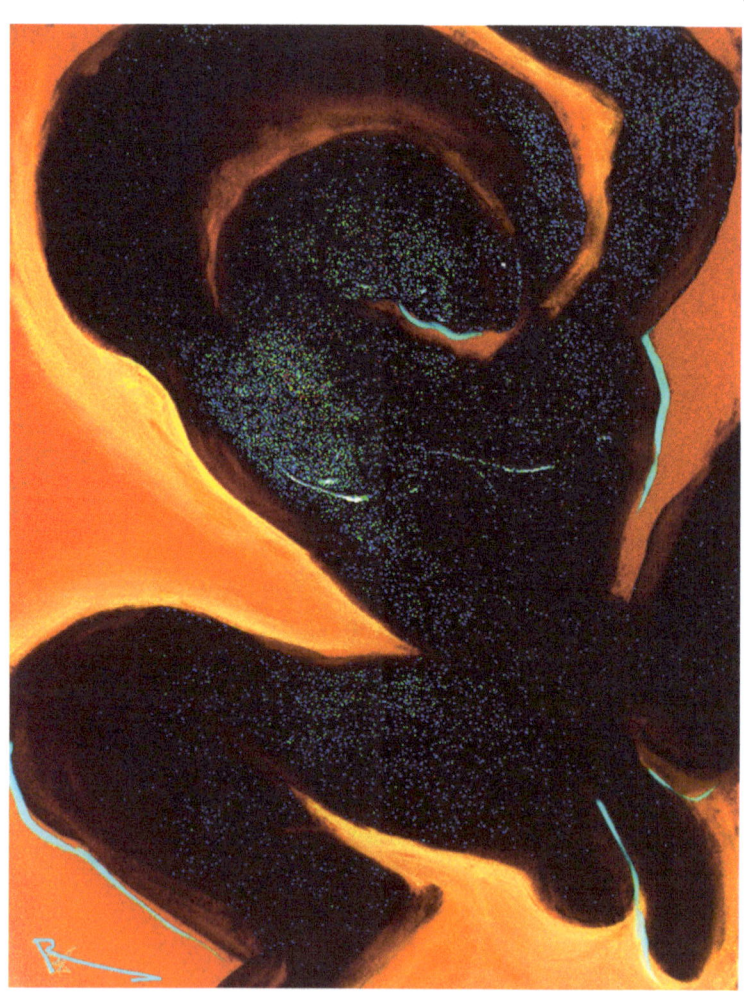

A well-built young preacher named Rex
worked out on his abs and his pecs.
    With heart all a flutter,
    a prayer he'd mutter,
then head to the steam room for sex.

———————————

There was a detective named Glover,
who bragged of the breasts of his lover,
    'til he saw the big stick
    on a handsome young dick,
and they spent the whole night under cover.

———————————

There once was a lawyer named Steve,
who kept many tricks up his sleeve.
    While down at the Y,
    he would ogle some guy,
and take home a sailor on leave.

———————————

A middle-aged preacher named Paul
had long ago answered the call,
    but another loud urge
    caused this pastor to merge
with his passion for sex, bacchanal!

———————————

A winsome young lad in his teens
was proud of his 501 jeans,
    'cause the bulge in the crotch
    swelled up quite a notch
as he watched several naked marines.

discovery

Oh, my sweet ass!

How long it took me to understand!

You were ugly, dirty,

and unworthy of attention.

I couldn't see you and

believed no one in his right mind

would want to look.

Eventually I became interested

and realize that there was more to you

than might meet the naked eye.

I poked a finger inside you.

Surprising sensation — not bad!

When I saw you in a mirror, I thought

how strange, but interesting!

I began to play with you,

incredible pink rosebud.

You responded, opening

to my finger, hungrily grasping

for lost friends.

I was estranged!

I've learned to play with you,

not poking fun, but tenderly

opening you to welcome me,

or some nice cock.

You were designed for fucking.

You are hungry for a good hard dick.

I will treat you to that banquet

as often as I can.

I promise.

love song

Too brief, that glorious time
holding each other,
laughing at follies,
weeping, recalling mistakes,
wondering together.
Dark coffee moments,
choosing to taste
with lips ripe as raspberries
of hard body, airy soul.

Sensuous lacy emotions
entangled in deep root connections.

Captured for late night reflection,
sacred hard-core tenderness
paces in my cage of memories,
longing to be free.
Where is he now?
Does he still know me by heart?
No answer comes —
a past beyond my reach,
that delectable hour
when we were young.

We held each other warm
those deepening and fragile nights,
dark, sweet, light, tart.
Would that ever be enough?

contributing artists

page 2: *Hands 3,* Alan Kaufman, 2011, pencil;
www.AlanKaufmanStudio.com, AlanKaufmanXYZ@gmail.com

page 8: *George Paris,* Todd Paris, 2008; photograph; ParisPics@Alaska.net

page 10: *Malakai and Mirror,* C. Hardwicke, 2005;
www.ChazHardwicke.com, Info@ChazHardwicke.com

page 14: *Maui,* Richard Koob, 2011, pastel on paper;
www.Kalani.com/RichardKoob, Richard.Koob@Kalani.com

page 16: *Blush,* Fernando Reyes, 2007, charcoal and pastel;
FReyesArt.com, FReyesArt@mac.com

page 18: *Warrior,* 2011, Andrew Ogus, mixed media;
Andrew-Ogus.artistwebsites.com, AndrewOgus@mindspring.com

page 20: *The Judgment of Paris 10,* 2010 Andrew Ogus, mixed media;
Andrew-Ogus.artistwebsites.com, AndrewOgus@mindspring.com

page 22: *Reclining Nude with Flowers*, C. Hardwicke, 1994, photograph;
www.ChazHardwicke.com, Info@ChazHardwicke.com

page 24: *Malakai, Sunset,* C. Hardwicke, 2005, photograph;
www.ChazHardwicke.com, Info@ChazHardwicke.com

page 26: *Hands #1,* Alan Kaufman, 2011, pencil;
www.AlanKaufmanStudio.com, AlanKaufmanXYZ@gmail.com

page 28: *Ethan,* Christopher Prouty,1999, graphite on illustration board;
Christoagogo@gmail.com

page 30: *Malakai, Doorway* C. Hardwicke, 2005, photograph;
www.ChazHardwicke.com, Info@ChazHardwicke.com

page 32: *Villa of the Mysteries* (detail), Andrew Ogus, 2011,
mixed media; Andrew-Ogus.artistwebsites.com,
AndrewOgus@mindspring.com

page 34: *Chris,* Charles H. Stinson, 1996, graphite on paper;
www.CharlesStinson.com, CHS@CharlesStinson.com

page 36, *Recline*, Christopher Prouty, 2007, graphite on
illustration board; Christoagogo@gmail.com

page 38: *Sitting Nude with Flowers*, C. Hardwicke, 1994, photograph;
www.ChazHardwicke.com, Info@ChazHardwicke.com

page 40: *Tattoo and Bands,* Alan Kaufman, 2010, charcoal:
www.AlanKaufmanStudio.com, AlanKaufmanXYZ@gmail.com

page 42: *Softening*, Trevor Southey, 1977, etching; www.TrevorSouthey.com, Trevor@TrevorSouthey.com

page 45: *Curious Glance*, Fernando Reyes, 2007, charcoal and conte; FReyesArt.com, FReyesArt@mac.com

page 46: *Reconciliation*, Trevor Southey, 1978, oil on board; www.TrevorSouthey.com, Trevor@TrevorSouthey.com

page 48: *Flight*, Trevor Southey, 1979, color intaglio; www.TrevorSouthey.com, Trevor@TrevorSouthey.com

page 50: *Lifting*, Trevor Southey, lithograph; www.TrevorSouthey.com, Trevor@TrevorSouthey.com

page 52: *Prodigal*, Trevor Southey, 1980, oil on board www.TrevorSouthey.com, Trevor@TrevorSouthey.com

page 54: *Flora*, Andrew Ogus, 2012, mixed media; Andrew-Ogus.artistwebsites.com, AndrewOgus@mindspring.com

page 56: *Falconetti*, Christopher Prouty, 2010, graphite on illustration board; Christoagogo@gmail.com

page 58: *Allen*, Tom Bianchi, photograph: www.TomBianchi.com, TWB@TomBianchi.com

page 60: *Deep in Thought, #2*, Alan Kaufman, 2004, charcoal; www.AlanKaufmanStudio.com, AlanKaufmanXYZ@gmail.com

page 62: *Ascending Torso*, Fernando Reyes, 2007, charcoal; FReyesArt.com, FReyesArt@mac.com

page 64: *The Oneiroii*, Andrew Ogus, 2012, mixed media; Andrew-Ogus.artistwebsites.com, AndrewOgus@mindspring.com

page 66: *Malakai, Asleep*, C. Hardwicke, 2005, photograph; www.ChazHardwicke.com, Info@ChazHardwicke.com

page 69: *Carlos*, Charles H. Stinson, 1996, graphite on paper; www.CharlesStinson.com, CHS@CharlesStinson.com

page 70: *Creation*, Rob Anderson, charcoal pencil and charcoal white on handmade paper; www.RobAndersonStudio.com, RobStudio@earthlink.net

page 72: *David*, Charles H. Stinson, 1996, graphite on paper; www.CharlesStinson.com, CHS@CharlesStinson.com

page 74: *Deep in Thought, #1*, Alan Kaufman, 2004, charcoal; www.AlanKaufmanStudio.com, AlanKaufmanXYZ@gmail.com

page 76: *Michael,* C. Hardwicke, 1995, photograph;
www.ChazHardwicke.com, Info@ChazHardwicke.com

page 78: *Kamapua'a,* Richard Koob, 1998, oil on paper;
www.Kalani.com/RichardKoob, Richard.Koob@Kalani.com

page 80: *Anonymous IV,* Fernando Reyes, 2011, charcoal and pastel;
FReyesArt.com, FReyesArt@mac.com

page 82: *Eka Pada Rajakapotasan*, C. Hardwicke, 1994, photograph;
www.ChazHardwicke.com, Info@ChazHardwicke.com